Y0-AGH-376

3 1385 00009 5685

WITHDRAWN

JF
Sil

Copy 2.   G16562

Silverstein, Shel

The missing pices meet
the Big O.

**GLENSIDE PUBLIC
LIBRARY DISTRICT**
Glendale Heights, Illinois 60137

Shel Silverstein

WITHDRAWN

The Missing Piece Meets the Big O

Harper & Row, Publishers

GLENSIDE PUBLIC LIBRARY DISTRICT
GLENDALE HEIGHTS, ILLINOIS 60137

to Joan

THE MISSING PIECE MEETS THE BIG O

Copyright © 1981 by Shel Silverstein

All rights reserved. No part of this book may be used or reproduced in any manner whatsoever without written permission except in the case of brief quotations embodied in critical articles and reviews. Printed in the United States of America. For information address Harper & Row, Publishers, Inc., 10 East 53rd Street, New York, N.Y. 10022. Published simultaneously in Canada by Fitzhenry & Whiteside Limited, Toronto.

First Edition

G16562

The missing piece sat alone...

waiting for someone
to come along
and take it somewhere.

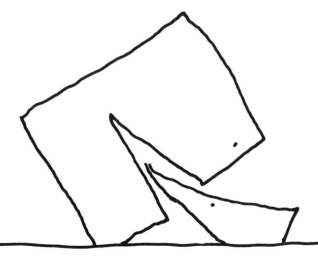

Some fit...

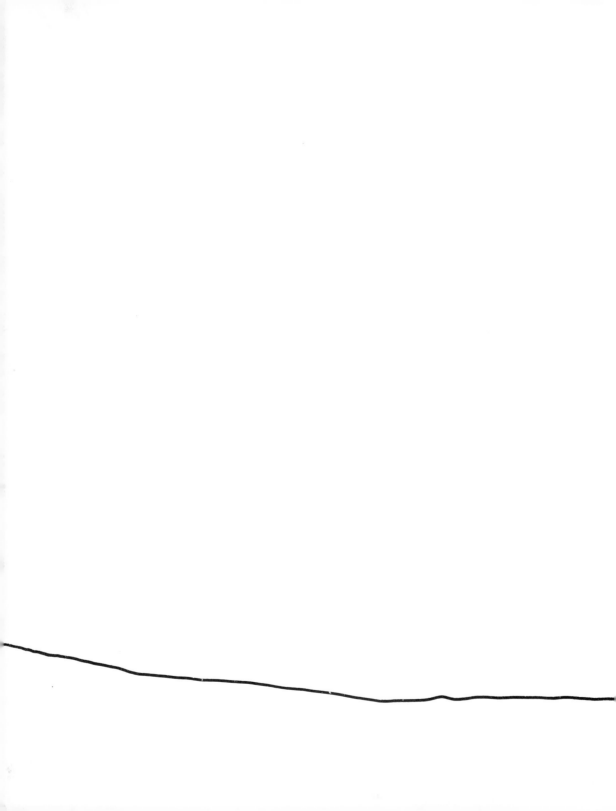

but could not roll.

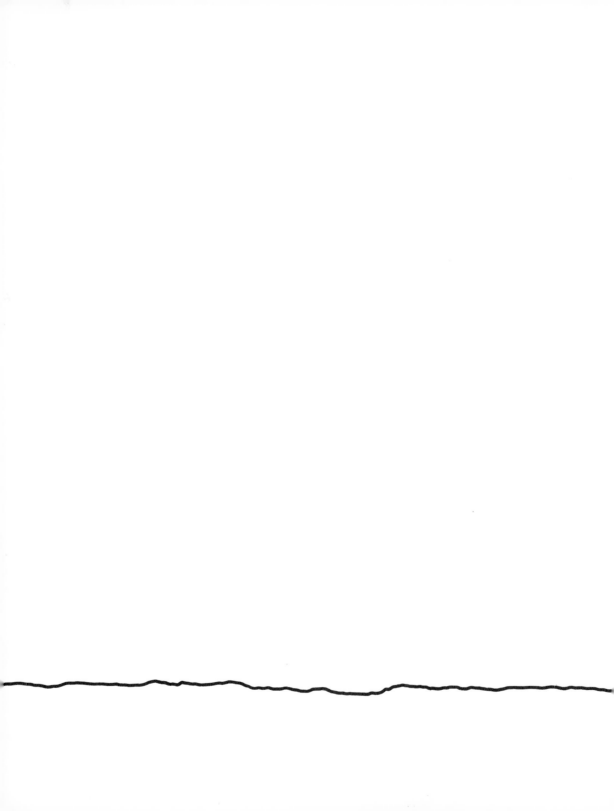

Others could roll
but did not fit.

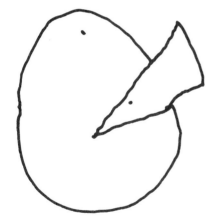

One didn't know a thing about fitting.

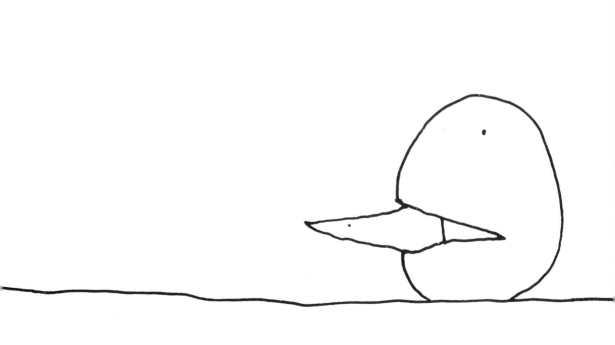

And another
didn't know a thing
about anything.

One was too delicate.

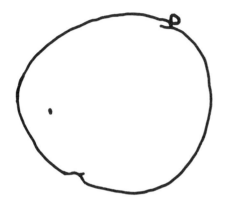

POP!

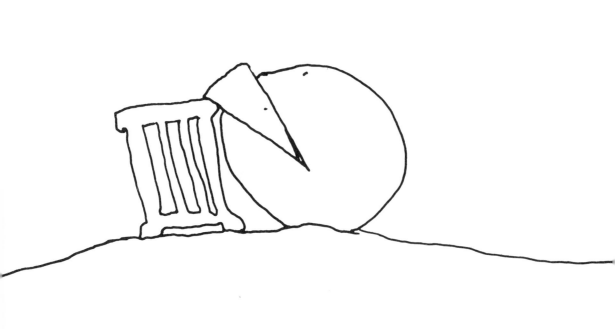

One put it on a pedestal…

and left it there.

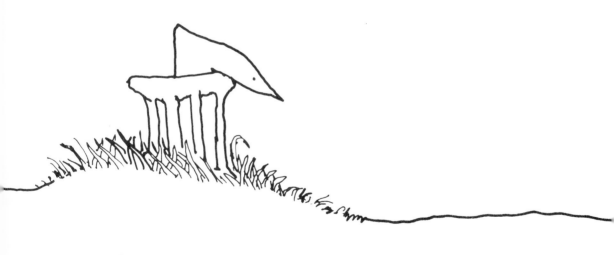

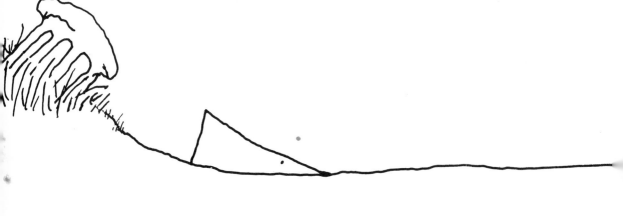

Some had too many pieces missing.

Some had too many pieces, period.

It learned to hide from the hungry ones.

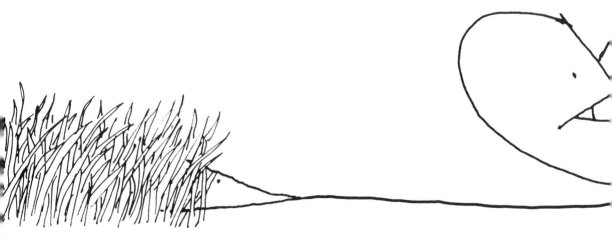

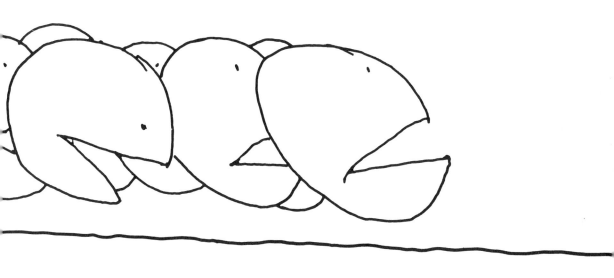

More came.

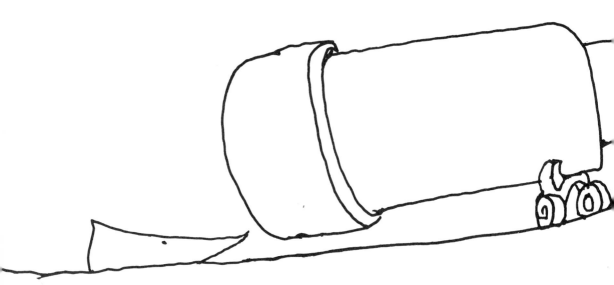

Some looked too closely.

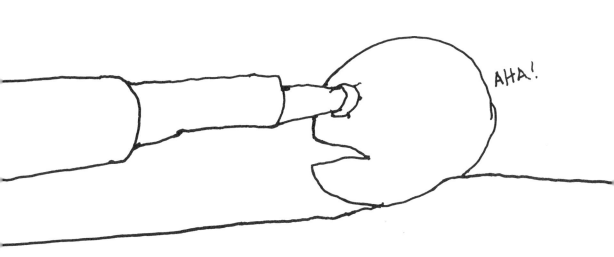

Others rolled right by without noticing.

HI..?

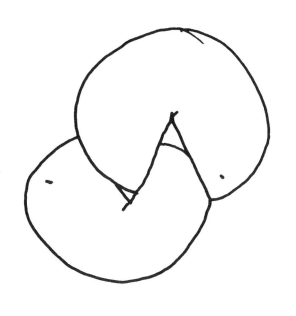

It tried to make itself
more attractive....

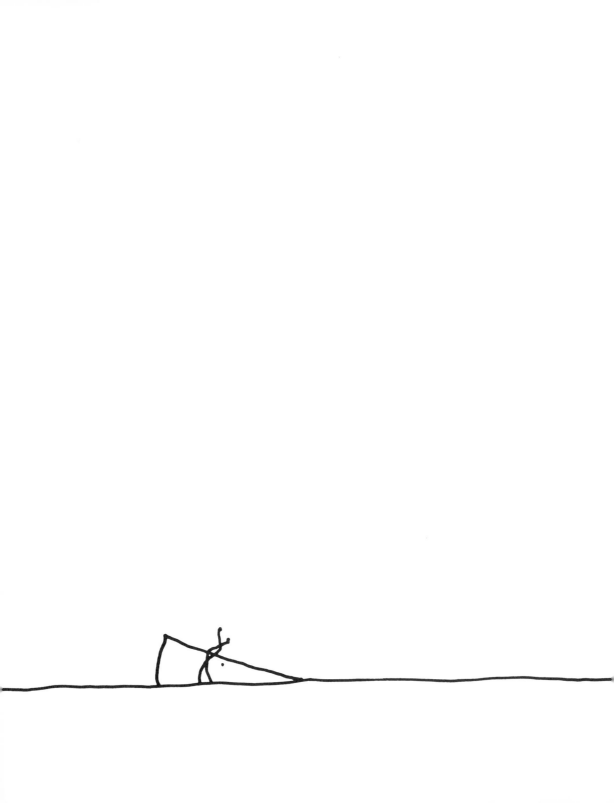

It didn't help.

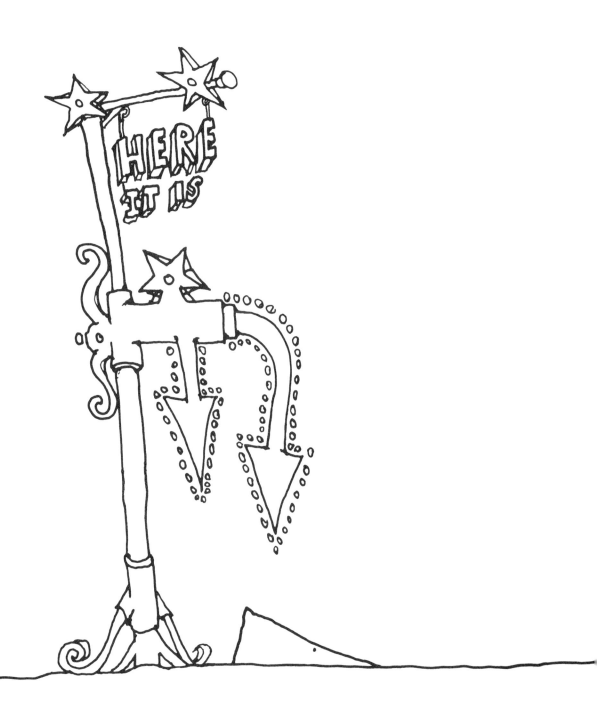

It tried being flashy

but that just frightened
away the shy ones.

At last one came along
that fit just right.

But all of a sudden…

the missing piece began to grow!

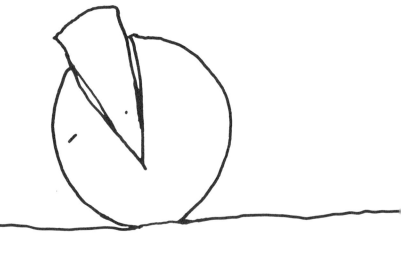

And grow!

"I didn't know
you were going
to grow."

"I didn't know it either,"
said the missing piece.

BYE...

"I'm lookin' for
my missin' piece,
one that won't
increase...."

SIGH....

And then one day,

one came along who looked different.

"What do you want of me?"
 asked the missing piece.

"Nothing."

"What do you need from me?"

"Nothing."

"Who are you?" asked the missing piece.

"I am the Big O,"
said the Big O.

"I think you are the one
  I have been waiting for,"
  said the missing piece.
"Maybe I am your missing piece."

"But I am not missing a piece,"
  said the Big O.
"There is no place you would fit."

"That is too bad," said the missing piece.
"I was hoping that perhaps
   I could roll with you...."

"You cannot roll with me,"
   said the Big O,
"but perhaps you can roll by yourself."

"By myself?
A missing piece cannot
roll by itself."

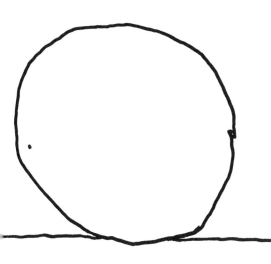

"Have you ever tried?"
asked the Big O.

"But I have sharp corners,"
said the missing piece.
"I am not shaped for rolling."

"Corners wear off,"
  said the Big O,
"and shapes change.
  Anyhow, I must say good-bye.
  Perhaps we will meet again...."

And away it rolled.

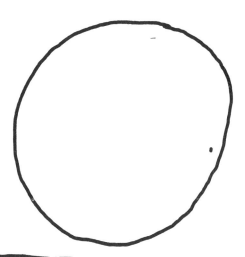

The missing piece
was alone again.

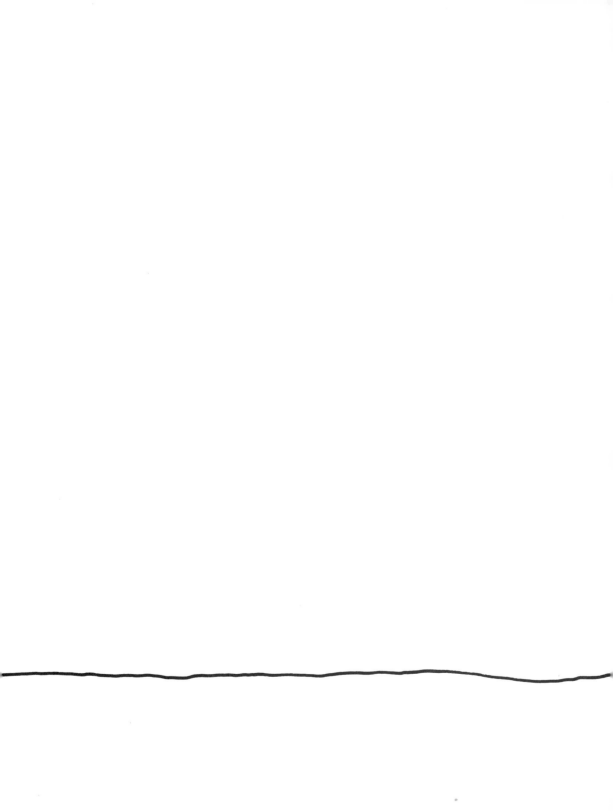

For a long time
it just sat there.

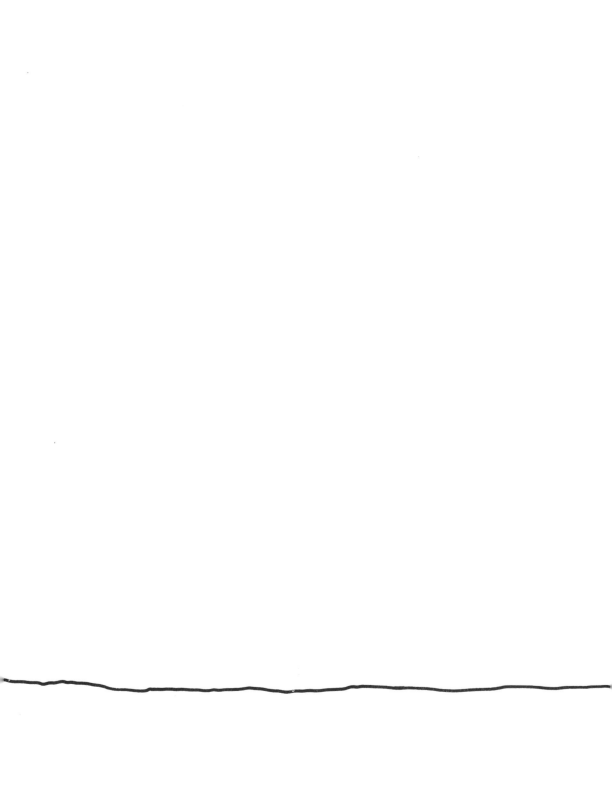

Then...
slowly...
it lifted itself up on one end...

...and flopped over.

PLOP!

Then lift…pull…flop…

it began to move forward....

And soon its edges began to wear off...

liftpullflopliftpullflop...

and its shape began to change…

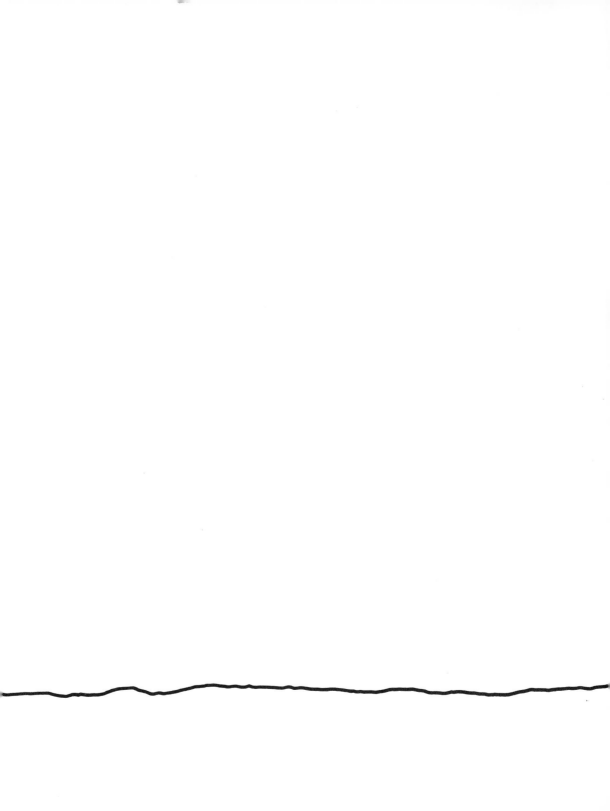

and then it was bumping instead of flopping...

and then it was bouncing instead of bumping...

and then it was rolling instead of bouncing ....

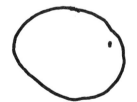

And it didn't know where
and it didn't care.

It was rolling!

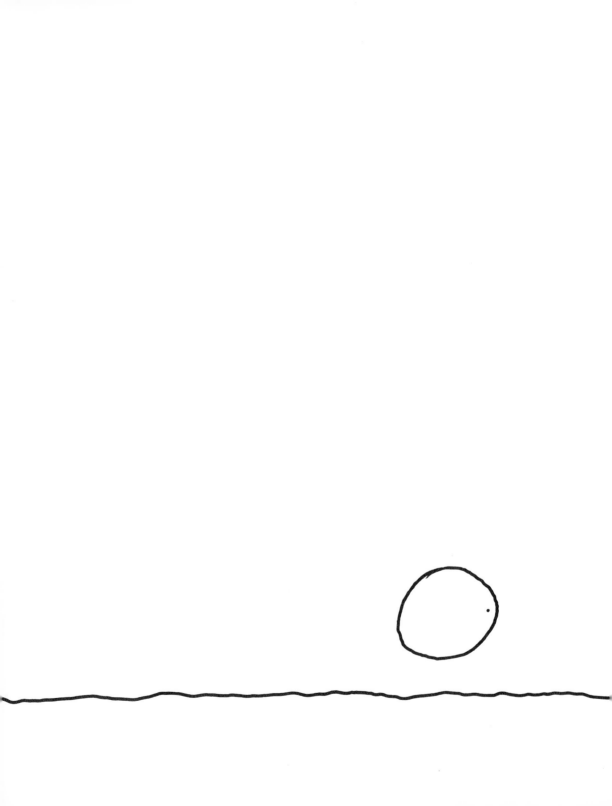

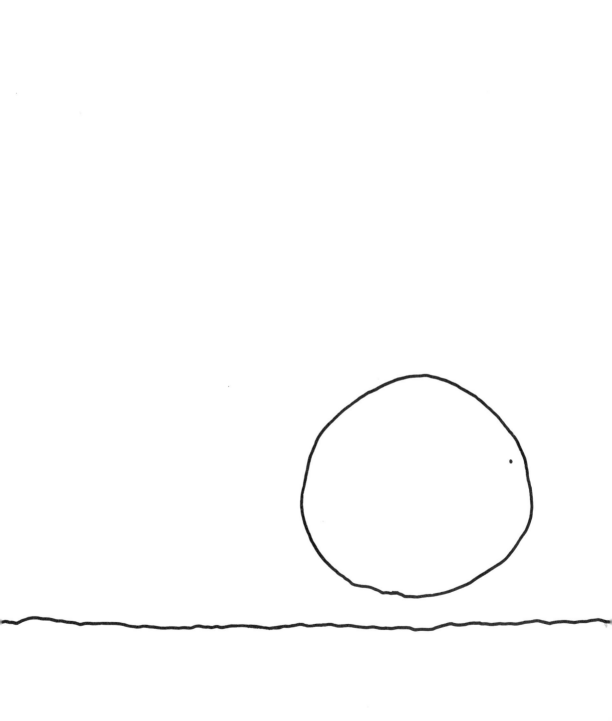